Mrs. S. Y. Leeds

September 1

1311 College St.

Bowling Green.

Kentucky.

The Enchanted Hill

..

A NOVEL

Gail saw Purdy swing the machine-gun into position.

THE
ENCHANTED HILL

BY
PETER B. KYNE

AUTHOR OF
NEVER THE TWAIN SHALL MEET,
KINDRED OF THE DUST,
CAPPY RICKS, ETC.

ILLUSTRATED BY
DEAN CORNWELL

NEW YORK
GROSSET & DUNLAP
PUBLISHERS

TO RAY LONG

This volume is dedicated in profound appreciation of his friendship, his ever ready aid, his able editorial criticism and boundless enthusiasm, without which the author would be singularly helpless

The Illustrations
consist of
A Frontispiece and a Centerspread
Reproduced in Color from the
Original Paintings by
DEAN CORNWELL

The Enchanted Hill

CHAPTER I

A ZEPHYR, light as an angel's breath, bore the incense of yerba santa and sage across the level gray stretches of El Valle de los Ojos Negros; yet from this labor it reserved sufficient strength to turn the fans of a light windmill, the mechanism of which, lacking lubrication, creaked, banshee-like, at each lazy revolution. Grasshoppers, mysteriously impelled to hop, decided instead to fly, and droned lugubriously down wind; the telephone and telegraph wires, strung on poles along the railroad right of way, hummed faintly, like distant harpsichords badly out of tune; in the sycamore trees flanking the thin trickle of water that was the Rio Hondo in time of freshet, two crows cawed sociably; a woodpecker rendered his very best imitation of a riveting machine. Save for this diapason of minor sounds there was silence in San Onofre.

San Onofre was accustomed to silence. It was a flag station in the heart of El Valle de los Ojos Negros, and over it and the cattle corrals and loading chute, the complaining windmill and a five-thousand-gallon water-tank kept guard. It boasted neither station agent nor station loafers; even the trains did not stop

1

there to take on water, for the windmill and tank had
been erected by the railroad company to supply water
to the transient herds of cattle held in the corrals for
car shipment, and for the horses and men who drove
the cattle thither.   Hence, except on those occasions
when the cow-men who ranged in El Valle de los Ojos
Negros and the public grazing lands in the forest reserve to the north and northeast drove their beef cattle
in for shipment, no human voice competed in San
Onofre with the zephyr, the grasshoppers, the crows
and the woodpecker.

Alone in San Onofre, Lee Purdy sat on the lip of the
loading chute and smoked a cigarette of his own manu-
facture.   Half an hour previous, a westbound freight
had picked up the ten carloads of steers he and his
men had loaded that day, and the range boss and six
men had accompanied the cattle to care for them en
route and check up on the weights when the shipment
should reach the stockyards in Los Angeles.   Stockyards were the most recent innovation in that boom-
throbbing metropolis, and it had occurred to Lee
Purdy to test the California market with New Mexico
range beef rather than the Kansas City or Chicago
markets, which had absorbed his brand in the past.

Joaquin José Ramon Oreña y Sanchez, alleged cook,
driving two mules hitched to the chuck wagon, had departed for the ranch headquarters immediately after
serving the midday meal.   To Joaquin, Lincoln Hallowell, the range boss, had entrusted his two best saddle-
horses for return to the ranch.   They were tethered at
the tail-gate of the chuck wagon.   The men who had
not accompanied the beef shipment had also departed,

heading home straight across country and herding before them the small *remuda* which had accompanied the drive to San Onofre; presently, after resting, smoking and cogitating, Lee Purdy would follow. Meanwhile he sat on the lip of the loading chute, his soul steeped in a gentle melancholy, his muscles relaxed in pleasing lassitude, his mind vaguely alive to the realization that he had prodded three hundred recalcitrant three-year steers up that loading chute and into the cattle cars that day.

He sighed. He was weary. A prodder of steers was he, and prodding steers was work designed by Providence for men strong in the arm and thick in the head; nevertheless, he, Lee Purdy, who was strong of arm but not thick of head, had performed his monotonous task without complaint, with a certain joy even, albeit there had not been any urgent necessity for his accompanying the drive to San Onofre, there to deplete his youthful vitality by prodding unwilling and suspicious Herefords up a loading chute. Link Hallowell, his range boss, could have got on very well without him.

The vague melancholy hereinbefore referred to, however, had its genesis not in rebellion at the character of his labors, but in a very definite realization of their futility. The shipment of steers he had just started westward would not reimburse him for the cost of production. With good fortune he might hope to net sixty-five dollars a head; and only a month previous, in New York, he had partaken of a small steak in a not very well-known restaurant and had paid therefor the sum of one dollar and twenty-five cents. He wondered now how many such steaks a clever butcher might be able to carve from the carcass of a thousand-pound steer.

"I ought to be a middleman," Lee Purdy told himself. "As a consumer and as a producer of beef I'm headed straight for economic ruin and vegetarianism."

He rested his tired body against the upright at the head of the loading chute and drowsed pleasurably in the mid-afternoon sunshine. The hum of the telegraph wires, the drone of the grasshoppers, the anesthesia of the clean, pure, aromatic air, lulled him little by little. He would rest awhile before commencing that forty-mile journey back to his ranch. He slept.

He awakened with a terrific start—the spasmodic reaction of one suddenly and violently plucked from the arms of Morpheus. Something had struck, with great force, the four-by-four-inch upright against which his head had been resting; the impact had been disturbingly close to his head. As he jerked upward, his ears registered on his sleep-drugged brain the clear, sharp crack of a high-power rifle; even as the thought came to him that somebody had deliberately used the Purdy head for a target, he lost his balance and fell in a ludicrous heap to the ground under the lip of the loading chute. Thereupon his guardian angel whispered to him to lie perfectly still.

He did. In about thirty seconds a second bullet ripped a hole through the shoulder of his canvas jacket and lost itself somewhere out on the sage. Still Purdy remained motionless, although a sharp, burning sensation on his shoulder informed him that the bullet, in its passage, had barely touched his skin and seared it.

He had but one chance in a million to live and he was taking advantage of that chance. Somebody was striving to kill him from ambush, and if the killer could be induced to believe he had accomplished his purpose, Lee Purdy hoped he might be inclined to ponder the futility of wasting additional ammunition on a corpse.

Lee Purdy knew that no murderer, fully convinced that he has killed his man at, say, four hundred yards, cares to walk that distance to view at close range the still and gory tribute to his skill. Wherefore, Purdy lay as he had fallen from the loading chute—on his left side, with his left arm thrust out under his head and his legs drawn up slightly. And as he lay thus, wondering if the bushwhacker would try a third shot for luck, two crows flew agitatedly over his head, and there was heard no longer their cawing or the *rat-tat-tat-tat-tat* of the woodpecker in the sycamore trees along the Rio Hondo. The Rio Hondo, a wide boulder-strewn wash perhaps three feet below the level of the surrounding country, paralleled the railroad tracks at a distance of about three hundred yards on the south. Purdy reasoned that the man who had shot at him had doubtless crept down this almost dry wash and hidden among the sycamores, since at the sound of his shooting the crows had abandoned their home-building and flown straight away from there.

There was no more shooting; nevertheless, for five minutes Lee Purdy remained as he had fallen, motionless. Then, quite distinctly, he heard a man say: "Get over there, boy!" Followed the sound of a smart slap.

"He's come to the conclusion he's done his job," Lee

Purdy decided. "He's mounting his horse to ride away; he's slapping the horse on the flank to make him swing away from some obstacle to his mounting. Well, here goes for the altars of the Purdy family!"

He rose and ran to his automobile across the railroad tracks. Following the fashion of so many cattlemen whose business necessitates their motoring frequently over lonely mountain roads, across sage and mesquite-studded plains and through timber where panther, bear, wolf or coyote, the cow-man's constant irritant, are frequently met, Lee Purdy carried, strapped to his spare tire in front, a cavalry rifle scabbard in which an army rifle, cut down to a sporting weapon and always loaded, nestled ready to his hand. After obtaining this rifle he dropped prone behind the steel railroad track which, perched on the ties, rose some twelve inches above the level of the ground on which Lee Purdy lay; with care the hundred-and-twenty-pound rail would afford him perfect protection.

He listened. Presently, above the thrum of the telegraph wires, he heard a slight sound that would have passed unnoticed by one whose every nerve was not strained to listen. It was the blow of a steel-shod hoof against a boulder in the wash of the Rio Hondo, and the sound came from east of where the man had spoken.

"He didn't see me get up," Lee Purdy exulted. "He was busy picking his way through the wash. But he'll come up out of the sycamores presently and halt for one last backward look to make certain. A fine sight at five hundred yards ought to fix that scoundrel's clock."

He adjusted his sights and decided that luck was with him, in that he would not have to make an allowance for windage, which is inconvenient when doing fast snap shooting. Then he drew the bolt, quietly slid a cartridge into the breech and waited, quite calm in his belief that he could not possibly be deceived in his estimate of human nature. Surely the scoundrel must know that in all that desolate lonely land there was no human being closer than Arguello, sixteen miles east. That knowledge would make him careless—inspire him with confidence.

The head of a roan horse appeared above the low fringe of sage along the northern bank of the Rio Hondo. It rose higher, turning as it rose, and presently horse and rider came into plain view. And even as Lee Purdy had assumed, the rider pulled up his horse, quartering toward San Onofre, and looked back for the thing he had left lying at the foot of the loading chute. He did not see readily that which he sought, so he raised his hand above his eyes to shade them from the westering sun while he looked again. . . .

As he watched the man slide slowly out of the saddle and fall beside his horse, Lee Purdy murmured, "I think I made a bull's-eye, but I'll take a leaf out of your book, my sweet Christian friend. It's a sign of hard luck when one doesn't make certain that an important job has been perfectly done. As some wiseacre once remarked, 'Genius is a capacity for taking infinite pains.' I'll stroll over and read your brand and earmarks."

He did, advancing briskly, his rifle at the ready, his glance never faltering from the man who lay so still beside the roan horse, now playfully nuzzling his late rider's body.

Purdy turned the man over on his back, and the two men gazed into each other's faces silently and thoughtfully. Then:

"I thought you'd come," said the wounded man, speaking with difficulty. "You were smart enough to fool me, so I figured if you were able to walk you'd do what I neglected to do—and that's make certain. Well, give me the mercy shot, as they say south of the Border."

Lee Purdy relieved the fallen man of a pistol in a shoulder holster under the latter's left arm. Next he opened the man's shirt and searched for the wound. He found it high up on the right side, with the point of exit under the right shoulder-blade. It had just missed the spine.

"I will be surprised if it develops that you broke any bones in your fall," he declared. "The horse stood fast enough and you slid off so slowly I would have fired again if I hadn't entertained so much respect for your horse. Why should anybody shoot a good honest horse?"

"Thanks. He *is* a good horse—an Irish hunter crossed with a Hermosillo range pony. Well?"

"I've drilled you through the right lung and made an extraordinarily clean job of it. I think you ought to get well. At any rate the chances are about even. Ever study the vagaries of the flight of a rifle bullet?"

"No."

Lee Purdy squatted on his heels and rolled another cigarette. "At short range—say up to two hundred yards—the bullet, after leaving the muzzle, has a twisty motion imparted to it by the lands, or what you call the rifling in the barrel. This causes the bullet to wobble, describing a tiny orbit as it speeds ahead, and if it reaches its target while this wobble is on, the result is a great jagged wound. At longer ranges, however, after the bullet has settled in its flight, it will, unless it strikes a bone, drill a neat small hole from entrance to exit. At extreme ranges, after the force of the bullet has been spent, it will begin to wobble again; then, if it hits a man, it will tear him up a bit. I dropped you at five hundred yards and if you have any particular desire to live your desire should be granted. You appear to be a tough, stringy sort of person."

The would-be assassin's dark, fierce eyes glowed somberly. "Are you playing with me before finishing your job?" he demanded.

"Certainly not. I'm not going to do anything to hasten your death."

"Why not? I tried my best to kill you."

"Well, I have never killed a wounded, helpless enemy, and if that experience can be avoided I prefer to avoid it. Of course, I tried my best to kill you five minutes ago, but that was in self-defense. I had to stop you or risk having you do a better job the next time you tried."

"But," said the stranger with a curiously frank grin, "you say you are not going to stop me. You appear to want me to live. Why? So I'll be grateful and tell you who hired me?"

"No. I do not expect you to snitch. If you've sold

yourself, stay sold. Be an honest killer, if that's your trade, but don't be a double-crossing crook."

This frank expression of a code evoked a chuckle from the wounded man. A slight hemorrhage stifled the chuckle almost instantly. When he could get his breath he said:

"I see. You're saving me to get hung, eh? Well, there were no witnesses, so how are you going to prove I tried to murder you? You can't convict a man on uncorroborated testimony. My word is as good as yours."

"You are an unimaginative ass. I haven't the slightest interest in you since I failed to wound you mortally. I'm going to bring my automobile over here, tuck you into the tonneau and run you down to the railroad hospital at Arguello. Have you got any money?"

"About two hundred and fifty dollars, Mr. Purdy."

"Well, then, pay your own hospital bills while it lasts. If it isn't enough I'll make up the deficit, and if you're foolish enough to die I'll give you Christian burial and write home to your folks a first-class lie regarding your demise, if you care to give me your home address."

"I don't understand you, Mr. Purdy. How do you know I won't try to earn my fee after I get out of hospital?"

Lee Purdy smiled a quiet, prescient little smile. "Well, if you're dog enough to do that I suppose that's one of the chances I'll have to take. Well, don't die, old settler, until I can get back here with my auto."

"Take my horse," said the killer affably.

"Thanks." Lee Purdy swung into the saddle and

galloped back to San Onofre, where he turned the horse into the cattle corral, and drove back in the automobile for his now thoroughly mystified passenger. With considerable difficulty he managed to get the fellow into the tonneau and stretched him out on the rear seat, with his long legs dangling over the side. Then, in low gear, Purdy drove away, breaking trail through the sage to the main road. It was a rough ride at best, and the wounded man was grateful when Purdy halted his car in the shadow of the tiny station at San Onofre.

"Well, what's the next move?" he demanded of Purdy.

"The California Limited is due in about fifteen minutes. I'm going to flag it and send you, in the baggage car, to Arguello."

"A limited train will not stop on flag."

"This one will," said Lee Purdy confidently. "I'll straddle the tracks with my auto and pretend I'm stalled."

"My name's Bud Shannon," his chance acquaintance volunteered. "You're a good fellow and I'm beholden to you."

"Pleased to make your acquaintance," Purdy said affably, and gave the wounded killer his hand. They stared at each other humorously. Then: "Any time you feel like giving up your present profession and tackling the hard, lonely life of a cow-hand, I'll give you seventy-five dollars a month, good board and the best lodging in New Mexico. I have a real bunk-house, not a kennel, and any foreman who can't make his men keep it clean can't be foreman."

"Mr. Purdy, I don't understand you a-tall."

"I'm not surprised. There are times, Bud, when I have difficulty understanding myself, and this is one of them. Want me to take your horse home with me and keep him until you're ready to fork him again?"

"By God, I don't understand you a-tall!" Bud Shannon repeated.

A plume of thin smoke showed over a low hill to the west. "Here comes the Limited," Purdy announced, and forthwith set his automobile astraddle of the tracks.

CHAPTER II

THE conductor, hurrying up the track, found the engineer and the fireman abusing Lee Purdy. They were casting thinly veiled aspersions upon his intelligence and impudence; to all of which Purdy paid not the slightest attention until the arrival of the conductor.

"Got a friend of mine here," he explained. "Shot accidentally. Take him into the baggage-car and drop him off at Arguello. Tell the station agent to see that he's sent to the railroad hospital and that Lee Purdy will guarantee the expenses."

"Whoa, boy," the conductor retorted. "You're a cool citizen of a mighty hot country, you are. I don't know Lee Purdy and the company doesn't trust him. Nobody rides on my train on any stranger's guarantee; so unless your friend has a valid pass, somebody will have to buy a ticket; otherwise I'll not attend the obsequies."

"I should have known there is no sentiment in a railroad company," Purdy retorted, and handed the conductor a dollar. The latter gravely made change, punched a receipt for a cash fare collected and handed it to Purdy, who tucked it in the killer's vest pocket. "Now, then," he suggested cheerfully, "let's go."

Bud Shannon was deposited on the floor of the baggage-car , but not until Lee Purdy had sacrificed a vil-

13

lainous old auto robe to furnish the desperado a pillow.
As he prepared to leave the car he slapped the Shannon
legs smartly and said, "Well, it might have turned out
worse for both of us, Bud. Take care of yourself, old-
timer. I'll see you at the railroad hospital at the
earliest opportunity."

Shannon reached for his would-be victim's hand.
"Mr. Purdy," he whispered, "if I knew your enemies in
this country I'd tell you who they were. If I ever find
out and provided I get over this, I'll kill 'em for you
and it won't cost you nothing. Compliments of Bud
Shannon."

"Well, so long, Bud. Pleasant green fields."

He stood on the station platform and watched the
Limited wind swiftly away and lose itself among some
low hills. Then he looked at his watch.

"Five o'clock," he soliloquized. "Guess I'll wash up
and get out of here. I'm as bloody as a butcher." He
went over into the corral and washed himself at the
watering trough, combed his hair with his fingers and
caught up Bud Shannon's horse. After loosening the
sixty-pound stock saddle he fastened a long horsehair
leading rope around the animal's neck and tethered the
horse to the rear of his automobile.

"Well, old boy," he addressed the animal as he
favored him with an affectionate rubbing under the
jaws, "it's up to you to step ten or twelve miles an
hour for an hour and a half."

Footsteps crossing the station platform caused him
to whirl and leap behind the automobile; on the instant
he drew the gun he had taken from Bud Shannon.
Upon his word, San Onofre was coming to life today.

He crouched behind the automobile, fully conscious of the fact that while the tonneau was no protection from bullets, at least it furnished fair camouflage for the target. A minute passed; and then a very pleasant, cool voice addressed him.

"You may put up your pistol, Mr. Purdy, and come out from behind your automobile. I give you my word of honor I am unarmed, and if I were I wouldn't dream of shooting you."

"Anybody with you?" Purdy demanded.

"No."

"I hope you're telling the truth. I'm coming out, but if anybody shoots at me it would be well to get me through the head with the first shot. I'll come a-fogging and I'll get you, even if you are a woman."

"Wait! I'll come to you. You're much too suspicious for comfort."

"Fair enough. I'll wait."

Footsteps crunched the sand; presently before Lee Purdy stood a girl. He stared at her amazed for about five seconds; then thrust his pistol down between his shirt and the waist-band of his trousers. He bowed a Castilian bow—sweeping in its completeness.

"I'm sorry," he said. "This happens to be an off day for me. I suppose, however, one may be permitted at least a day a year to indulge himself in suspicion."

"You *are* a bit jumpy," the stranger assured him soberly. "However, I dare say your reasons are sound and sufficient."

He nodded. "You addressed me by name. May I remind you that I am desolated at my ignorance of your identity?"

"I am Miss Gail Ormsby of Los Angeles. Mr. Todd was to meet me here."

"Oh, so you dropped off the Limited here? I didn't see you alight."

The girl nodded. "You were otherwise engaged."

"And that engine crew abused me for flagging the train with my automobile, when all the time the greasy rascals knew the train was going to stop at San Onofre anyhow. So you were expecting Mr. Ira Todd to call for you here?"

The girl nodded again.

"Well, Miss Ormsby, he isn't going to keep his engagement. He drove in from his ranch to Arguello last night. I saw him there this morning and shortly after that he was taken ill."

"Oh, I'm so sorry! What is the matter with him?"

Lee Purdy hung his head and slowly scuffed a hole in the dirt with his boot toe. He admitted finally: "A worthy citizen of Arguello found it necessary to bend an iron bar over Mr. Ira Todd's head, Miss Ormsby. I think he fractured the Todd skull; at any rate, the last I saw of Ira Todd the pupils of his eyes had contracted to mere pin-points, and it is my personal although unprofessional opinion that Ira Todd has concussion of the brain."

"How perfectly dreadful!" Miss Ormsby's fine eyes and finer features puckered with horror. "What has been done to his assailant?"

"He has been congratulated by a number of solid citizens and cursed and threatened by other citizens not quite so solid."

"I do believe you are Ira Todd's assailant."

"Hot, hot, red-hot!" he replied lightly. "You're on my trail, Miss Ormsby; you'll tree me in a minute. However, you're just a *trifle* wrong. Ira Todd was my assailant. He went into a restaurant in Arguello and there in a loud voice made statements derogatory to my honor. I was breakfasting there at the time. Unfortunately for him, the restaurant happens to be owned and operated by a very good friend of mine, a Chinaman who drifted down into this country about five years ago suffering from tuberculosis. I found the poor devil hungry and broke in Arguello and without a friend, so I had him come out to my ranch and stick around until he got well. Then I loaned him five hundred dollars to get into business in Arguello. He has repaid the money but still feels indebted to me, so when the unfortunate Ira spoke out of his turn in Chan's presence and in Chan's restaurant, Chan just naturally busted him with a short iron slice-bar he uses to poke up the charcoal under his steak broiler. What makes you think I discommoded you by ruining Ira?"

"Because you're quite gory now and I saw you help put a wounded man aboard the train. Somebody said he had been shot and was dying."

"Maybe so," murmured Lee Purdy. "I fear the best but hope for the worst."

"You told the conductor he had been shot accidentally. Who shot you accidentally?" And she tapped her shoulder significantly.

Purdy laughed softly. "This is the most accidental country I ever knew, Miss Ormsby. However, I haven't been shot. Almost, but not quite. Where are you bound?"

"For the Box K Ranch."

"Oh! I never would have guessed it."

The gentle irony in his soft voice was not lost on the girl. She stared at him haughtily.

"This your first visit to our country, Miss Ormsby?"

"Yes."

"Did I understand you to say you were from Los Angeles?"

The girl nodded, without abating her cool scrutiny of him.

"I suppose," he resumed presently, "I'll have to be Ira Todd's attorney-in-fact and do for him and in his name, place and stead all of those things which he would or could do if personally present. That car of mine is sound and seaworthy, although it looks like original sin; there's room for you in the front seat and for all of your baggage in the tonneau. I'm a safe, sane, conservative driver, and I am at your service."

"I'm not so certain that I ought to accept your invitation, Mr. Purdy, although I thank you for it. I think you're a cool sort of desperado. I'm quite certain you and that wounded man have been shooting at each other because—because—well, when I saw that you hadn't noticed me sitting quietly on that bench yonder, I started toward you. And at the sound of my first footfall on this platform you turned like a flash and reached for the pistol in your waistband and hid behind this motorcar."

"The witness declines to answer any accusations upon the ground that he may incriminate himself." He glanced at his watch. "Five minutes after five," he announced, "and all members of the desperadoes' union, knock off at five. Better take a chance and ride with me."

"Somebody else may call for me in Ira Todd's place."

"Scarcely probable, unless Ira issued instructions to that effect before my friend Chan stretched him. And even if somebody should call for you I wouldn't think of permitting you to go with him; no, that was a stupid way to express it—I mean I wouldn't think of permitting him to—ah—serve you. However, I'm certain no such regrettable contingency will arise."

"You are much too certain of yourself, Mr. Purdy. I shall *not* accompany you—at least, not willingly."

He appeared to accept her decision as final. "Then may I have the pleasure of freighting your baggage for you? Whoever calls here for you will arrive in a flivver, and flivvers and that wardrobe trunk of yours were never meant to be coupled in the betting. Still, if you think I might steal your trunk, you have my word that it will be quite safe if left on the platform. Very few white men are around here lately."

She repressed with difficulty a desire to laugh. "In that case it is scarcely kind to trouble you with my baggage."

"A lady's slightest whim is, to me, a command. I am bound for Arguello. If I do not meet anybody on the road coming to fetch you I'll engage somebody in Arguello with a car to do it. However, I have to proceed slowly, because I am going to lead this horse behind my car. I imagine it will be about three, perhaps four, hours before anybody comes for you, and San Onofre is a very lonely place after dark. The altitude is about two thousand feet here and after the sun sets the nights are bitterly cold. Coyotes howl in the sage hereabouts and once in a while a lobo wolf drops around to see if anybody has left a sick steer in the loading corral. However, since you cannot trust me, of course——"

"Pick up the marbles, Mr. Purdy. You win," Miss Ormsby, of Los Angeles, interrupted, bravely enough but with a suspicious eagerness.

Lee Purdy bowed acknowledgment of her surrender.

CHAPTER III

THAT was a long and memorable drive to Arguello. The horse did not take kindly to being led behind an automobile, and it required very slow going at first to win the animal's confidence; he showed a disposition to be towed rather than led, and once, in his terror and bewilderment, he half turned and did a devil's tattoo with his heels on the rear of the tonneau.

"It's an awful thing to have been born cursed with an obliging disposition," Lee Purdy mourned. "Here you observe the spectacle of another man's horse kicking holes in my automobile."

"If he succeeds in kicking any paint off your automobile I'll send him a sack of oats," Miss Ormsby answered crisply. "Another dent or two cannot possibly make any difference."

Purdy nodded. "I do not yearn for new and shiny automobiles as I used to," he admitted. "This one has a good motor; it gets me where I want to go."

"Isn't this your horse then, Mr. Purdy?"

"No, it belongs to the wounded man you saw me put aboard the train."

"Who was that man?"

"I don't know. Never met him before."

"I had an idea he was a friend of yours. I heard you instruct the conductor to tell the station agent at Arguello to send the man to the railroad hospital and

that you would guarantee the bill." Purdy had no answer to that. "Well?" the girl persisted.

"Well, what?"

"I'm bursting with curiosity. Why did you guarantee the hospital bill of a total stranger and then
take charge of his horse?"

"I didn't know what else to do. The man has a
chance to recover and I couldn't very well leave him to
die all alone out in the sage, could I? Besides, this
horse looks good to me. Good saddle and bridle, too.
If that man dies and nobody calls for his horse and
outfit I suppose I may, with entire propriety, keep it.
Moreover, I'm entitled to security for that hospital bill,
am I not?"

"I prefer to think you have done all this because you
are magnanimous—or sorry you shot that man."

"How do you know I shot him?"

"While you were fussing with that horse a little
while ago I pulled your rifle half-way out of the scabbard and looked in the breech. There is an empty
shell in it."

He turned toward her and favored her with a frank,
appreciative smile, but made no verbal comment on her
perspicacity. "How do you know you were looking at
my rifle?" he parried.

"Because his is in the tonneau! His belt is there
also, and I noticed two vacancies. So I suspect he
shot at you twice. I suspect too that you took that
pistol away from him, otherwise you would have a
holster for it. It must be inconvenient to wear it inside
the band of your trousers, like a professional killer."

"What do you know about professional killers?"

"They're all over Hollywood," she replied lightly. "You can't fool me on Wild West stuff. I have been raised too close to motion pictures. Out in my country we're fed up on it."

"I think I approve of you—quite," said Lee Purdy.

"I think I might be induced to approve of you if you were more communicative. Why did Ira Todd speak ill of you?"

"Well, you see, Miss Ormsby, Ira doesn't like me."

"What did you do to cause him to dislike you?"

"I wear these riding breeches and boots and a wrist watch and a necktie and I use a handkerchief. I suppose Ira Todd could put up with these weaknesses of mine, but I strain his good nature by brushing my teeth and bathing frequently between the spring and the fall round-ups. So Ira thinks I'm a dude and tells everybody I am."

The girl laughed, and her silvery cachinnation tinkled pleasantly on ears long since attuned to the heartier and less refined laughter of the local belles. "I wonder what you think of Ira Todd?" she ventured. But Lee Purdy was silent, and she told herself she liked him for that.

However, like the majority of her sex, Gail Ormsby was curious.

"Why did the owner of this horse shoot at you, Mr. Purdy?"

"I forgot to ask him the exact amount, Miss Ormsby, but I surmise he did it for a sum in the neighborhood of two hundred dollars. The market price for removing objectionable persons, according to the last quotation I had, is two hundred dollars."

"And the man was not your enemy? He tried to kill you to earn a fee?" Horror and incredulity were expressed in her face and voice.

"I have his word for it, Miss Ormsby; I know of no reason why he should lie about it. I didn't ask him about his business. His admission was quite voluntary."

"How perfectly atrocious! Why, I thought the Wild West survived only in Hollywood!"

"There is no Wild West, and I doubt very much if the West was ever much wilder than the East. I can engage a gangster in New York or Chicago to remove an objectionable person for a sum as low as fifty dollars. Out here, however, our professional killers have some professional pride. They believe that the laborer is worthy of his hire and they will *not* work for scab wages. I honor them for it."

She glanced at him quickly, but his face was solemn to the point of sadness. "You appear to regard this attempt upon your life as a very trifling affair, Mr. Purdy," she pursued.

He nodded. "Life is a very trifling affair, Miss Ormsby. Some years back I learned how not to take it seriously. My life is quite heavily insured, and I'm much more valuable dressed than on the hoof."

"Are you a fatalist?"

"Oh, no, indeed! A fatalist is one who believes that what will happen will happen, whereas I know from experience that what will happen may be indefinitely delayed if one exercises a little horse-sense."

"You must have an implacable enemy in this country, Mr. Purdy."

"Your Mr. Ira Todd is the only man here who evinces an active dislike of me. However, Todd didn't hire that killer."

"I'm sure he didn't. Really, Mr. Purdy, he wouldn't."

"Of course he wouldn't!" Purdy's voice carried a razor edge of sarcasm.

"I'm glad to hear you say so positively that he did not hire that loathsome reptile. Do you know who did?"

"I do not, Miss Ormsby."

"Why does Ira Todd dislike you, Mr. Purdy? Please tell me the real reason."

Lee Purdy's grave face lighted with a grim smile. "Oh," he answered lightly, "Ira doesn't dislike me half as much as he does my idea of dress, and the fact that while I am of this country, nevertheless I am an alien. Remember what old What's-his-name said: 'We hate people because we do not know them, and we do not know them because we hate them.' "

"Do you dislike Ira Todd?"

"Certainly. I dislike him exceedingly. Do you like him, Miss Ormsby?"

"I have never met Ira Todd," she answered.

"Well, when you do you'll like him. Todd is a fairly presentable chap. He's a good cow-man and a good ranch manager of the old school; he has a host of friends in this country, and once he served a term as sheriff, cleaned up the office and ran some twenty undesirable characters off to greener pastures. He is good-looking and courageous."

"Then why do you dislike him exceedingly?"

"Must I answer that question?" he rebuked her gently.

"Sorry!" she answered. "I didn't mean to be nosey."

"Todd's is not a negative character," he went on, ignoring her apology. "I told you he had a host of friends. It is to his credit that he has, also, a host of enemies."

The girl smiled. She mistrusted this man exceedingly, for all his apparent good breeding. He was too cool, quite too sure of himself, too commanding. Nevertheless, he had a way with him—a way of facing facts and issues.

"I think," she said presently, "that eventually you and Mr. Todd will grow to be good friends."

"I'm glad you're beginning to like me," he replied gratefully.

She bit her lip. She could have pinched him for that speech. She cast about in her mind for something to say to that—something that would put him in his place; but before she could wither him the golden moment for doing so had passed. Perhaps, too, it would be just as well to ignore him. In a sense she was his guest. He had rescued her from a terrible predicament and if he chose to trade on her sense of obligation to him . . .

At a distance there came to the girl the faint hum of an airplane motor. Simultaneously she and Purdy glanced skyward.

"Mail plane or army?" Miss Ormsby queried.

"Neither. It's mine. I recognize the purr of my own bus."

He stopped the car, got out and stood in the trail,

waving a white handkerchief. The plane circled lower and lower until it was not more than five hundred yards overhead, when apparently the aviator recognized Purdy, for at once he commenced opening and closing his muffler in a most inexplicable manner. Purdy stood with bent head listening until the aviator ceased his peculiar actions; then the girl saw her strange host wave both arms skyward in a gesture that even she knew meant "Very well, I understand."

Immediately the airplane zoomed upward and disappeared into the northeast. Purdy climbed back into his car and resumed their journey. He drove in silence for ten miles; then, suddenly aware of his lack of companionship, he turned to Gail Ormsby.

"That was my mechanician. He had a message for me, so he flew over and gave it to me in the international code—opening and closing his muffler. Just dots and dashes, Miss Ormsby, and if nobody is hurrying one, one can make them with a motor or a telegraph instrument."

"We are not very far from the Mexican Border, are we, Mr. Purdy?"

"About an hour by airplane."

"I know now what you are," she challenged. "You're a bootlegger—operating with automobile and airplane, and running contraband liquor across the Border."

"Well, it will not be necessary to tell the world about it, Miss Ormsby."

"I'll not. Nevertheless, Mr. Purdy, it does seem a great pity that a man of your obvious good breeding and education should stoop to that illicit traffic, with

its shootings and killings, its dodging and hiding, its
bribery and corruption. There are so many other
ways for an intelligent man to make money."

He laughed softly. "It's so many long years since
I've been lectured about my morals," he declared.
"Please go on. I like it."

She flushed at his raillery. "Do you fly airplanes,
too? You said that was your own bus."

"Oh, yes, I fly them!"

"I dare say you learned during the war."

"Right you are."

"Were you an enlisted man or an officer?"

"I was an officer. In fact, I am an officer still. I'm
a major of aviation in the Officers' Reserve Corps."

"You are presumed to be a gentleman, too, aren't
you, Major Purdy?"

"Please," he pleaded, "do not be too hard on me."

"I cannot understand the character of a man who
will risk his life to serve his country in war but who in
time of peace risks his life with equal carelessness to
break his country's laws and make a few dirty dollars
in poisonous whisky."

"I can understand such fellows very well, Miss
Ormsby."

"Do you mean to tell me you defend your actions?"

"Indeed, I do. You see, I'm not a bootlegger."

"Then why didn't you say so in the first place?
You led me to believe——"

"I didn't do anything of the sort. Nobody has to
lead you to believe anything. You are very observant
and deductive—so you jump to conclusions."

"But you permitted me to lecture you——"

"I liked it. If you hadn't been interested in me you wouldn't have lectured me."

She flushed and her eyes sparkled dangerously. She disliked being drawn into traps and having fun poked at her by total strangers. "Well, what *is* your business?" she demanded.

"I'm a cattleman, Miss Ormsby."

"You are the first cattleman I have ever seen who wore park riding boots, English riding breeches and tailor-made shirts. Do you herd your cows from an airplane?"

"Please do not be provoked, Miss Ormsby. I'm an alien in this country and I fly around it in an airplane a great deal for the reason that I like to keep in practice, it saves me much valuable time, I avoid traveling rough, uncared-for roads and I like to give the natives of the country something to talk about, something to look forward to. They expect to see me crash and perish one day, and when that happens they'll say, 'Serves the durned fool right. Why didn't he stick to hosses?'"

The girl sighed. "I think you're a most unusual person," she admitted reluctantly.

"And you're glad I'm not a bootlegger?"

"I would be glad to be certain nobody is a bootlegger."

"I would have preferred a more definite reply, but never mind."

"Have you ever crashed?"

"A couple of times."

"Get hurt?"

"Roughed up a little once."

"But you must find it quite expensive maintaining and repairing an airplane."

"Not at all. I have half a dozen ships at my ranch. When one is out of business, I fly another."

"Indeed!"

"They were supposed to be fighting planes in nineteen seventeen, but they were demoded in nineteen nineteen, so I bought six of them from the government for two hundred and fifty dollars each. I have six spare four-cylinder motors that cost me a hundred and fifty dollars each, so I expect to fly for quite a few years. A hundred miles an hour is fast enough when nobody is pursuing one. I attract considerable attention and criticism flying around this country. It is said that I frighten the cows and their milk turns sour."

"Do you ever fly over the Box K Ranch?"

"Very frequently. There is an alfalfa field just below the ranch-house. It is excellent landing ground and my plane doesn't hurt the alfalfa; but Ira Todd thinks it does, so I cannot land there any more and that is an inconvenience. You see, I am the volunteer aerial patrol over the Cuyamaca National Forest."

"Why, I thought our national forests were patrolled by the air forces of the United States Army, Major."

"They used to be, but this year the United States Army Air Force is short of gasoline and lubricating oil. Congress is in a parsimonious mood except in the purchase of votes. Five billion dollars' worth of our navy is rusting to disuse because we cannot afford men to care for the ships, and the last stand of public timber in our country may risk loss by fire in order that we may save a few thousand dollars' worth of gasoline. Our so-called economy has so crippled the air forces that we haven't flyers enough to go around. They are needed at flying fields to act as instructors. Consequently, I've taken over the Cuyamaca patrol myself."

"You amazing man! Who pays for your oil and gasoline?"

"Oh, I pay for it myself when I have to! Last year the cattlemen who have grazing permits in the forest reserve donated about two thousand dollars to the cause, but this year the cattlemen are in a bad, bad way financially, so I'm not asking them for a donation which they cannot afford."

"Do you make a daily patrol?"

"Good gracious, no! I am much too busy a man. I do try very hard, however, to get around three times a week. The forest ranger service is always on the job, it is tremendously efficient and tremendously loyal, and between them and me we've been pretty lucky. Haven't had a sizable fire in three years, although we would have had eight if I hadn't discovered them in embryo while on patrol and given the rangers prompt warning."

"How do you warn them?"

"I circle low over the ranger station and honk my horn until I attract the attention of the ranger; then I drop him a message. He warns the other stations by telephone. It's a heap of fun."

"I think it's a heap of work—hard, expensive, dangerous work."

"Well, you don't mind that after you get interested in the forest ranger service, Miss Ormsby. There is

one department of the federal service where there is a
minimum of graft, politics and self-seeking; it's a hard
and lonely life and only a certain type of man will
stand it. It is, however, the only life such men can
live happily. They are interested in nothing except
trees and animal life—nature-lovers, every one of
them. They are underpaid, unappreciated, unknown;
their world is the Forest Reserve area they are told off
to guard. Soldiers die in battle. So do forest rangers,
and when they do they die harder and more dreadful
deaths than soldiers. Had a good friend of mine
burned to death last year. His widow is the lookout
on San Buenaventura. Spends her young life ten miles
from human society, looking after a baby and a tele-
scope."

"And you enjoy playing the game with the forest
ranger service, even to the extent of paying a high
price to participate?"

"Oh, I'm not exactly a philanthropist, Miss
Ormsby! I hold a distinctly worth-while grazing permit
in the Cuyamaca. It is my summer range for five thousand cattle. My winter range, farther down, contains
a hundred thousand acres of fair grazing land. Seven
thousand acres of it lie in the upper end of the valley
of the main Rio Hondo, and that's where I cut my wild
hay. Of course a fire in the Cuyamaca Reserve can
spread to my winter range and burn up all the hay I
cut and stack during the summer to tide me over a hard
winter. I hate to have a starving cow ask me for hay
and be told to help herself to sage-brush—all because
the hay has been burned in a fire started by some igno-
rant, careless, lazy, unappreciative hunter or camper

who neglects to put out his camp-fire," he told her.

"That must be, indeed, a sad experience."

"Cows are so forlorn and forgiving when they're starving that it makes the experience all the sadder," he went on. "I tell you, Miss Ormsby, when a simple, confiding old cow puts all of her faith and trust in you and you go back on her, you feel mighty mean about it."

"The Box K Ranch runs cattle in the Cuyamaca," the girl informed him.

"A few hundred head," he replied indifferently.

They topped a long high hill; afar the cluster of lights that marked Arguello shone through the darkness. "We leave El Valle de los Ojos Negros here," Purdy announced.

"What does that mean?"

"It means the valley of the black eyes."

"How queer! What is the name symbolic of?"

"There are half a dozen little shallow lakes in the upper end of that valley. They are invaluable as drinking places for cattle. Viewed from the hills late in the day, two of these lakes nestling in that valley look like two dark eyes set in a vast and ugly human face. Then, too, many men have quarreled over that water and black eyes have frequently resulted. So the Mexicans hereabouts have coined for the valley the title of El Valle de los Ojos Negros." He leaned toward her anxiously. "I hope you're not afraid to make this journey with me, Miss Ormsby."

"No, I'm not afraid of you, Major Purdy. I made up my mind to that back at San Onofre. I had to trust you then, so I decided to trust you all the way."

where he is met by the Mexican, who is mounted on one of the best, fastest and toughest cow-horses in New Mexico, and leading another. With a prayer of gratitude to his heathen gods, the Chinaman mounts and the friends go away from there in a very great hurry. While nobody in Arguello is desirous of lynching the Mexican, nevertheless the said Mexican realizes that, having in a moment of impulsiveness promised the Chinaman a horse and made good on that promise, he is going to be decidedly unpopular if he remains in Arguello to face the disappointed mob. He realizes, too, that he is but a lowly Mexican ranch cook whom nobody loves, but the Chinaman is a friend of his boss, and therefore it is up to him to do exactly what his boss would do under the same circumstances.

"Why, then, remain in Arguello to defend his actions against superior numbers? There exists but one reason. This chuck wagon and equipment, these mules were all entrusted to his keeping. He is responsible for them. He dare not abandon them. But, no, señor! *Caramba*, no! Señor Purdy will pass within the hour. He will stop at the restaurant for his supper. He will observe the outfit standing at the side of Main Street, and he will institute an investigation and discover things. Forthwith he will engage some worthy citizen to take up the uncompleted labors of his servant, Joaquin José Ramon Oreña y Sanchez, and see to it that the outfit reaches the ranch safely. And, having wotted the which, Joaquin José Ramon and his friend from China faded away into the hills."

Purdy ceased flapping his hands and sat up with a little cry of fright and surprise. "Have I been talking

wildly, Miss Ormsby?" he demanded anxiously "I
think I've been in a trance or something."

"The reputations of the seers of this world are safe
in your hands, Mr. Purdy. In our own quaint
American patois, you said a mouthful. Now, when and
where do we eat?"

"I do not know," Purdy answered cheerfully, "but
the ravens fed Elijah, and inasmuch as I think I have
more brains than a raven, you just hold the thought
that I'll feed you." He swung his car in back of the
chuck wagon and got out. The girl saw him rummag-
ing around in the bed of the wagon and flashing his
electric torch among a number of bundles and boxes
there. Presently he returned to her carrying a gunny-
sack half full of something and he put it in the tonneau.

"The citizens of Arguello and surrounding territory
may riot, threaten, destroy property and lynch folks,
but they have one great, triumphant virtue," he announced. "They are honest. Nobody ever sinks so
low as to steal things from one's automobile or chuck
wagon. I suspected that Joaquin José Ramon Oreña
y Sanchez might have some grub left in the chuck box,
and sure enough he had. Now, if you will sit here
quietly until I can find a Mexican who will engage to
drive this outfit home, I'll be your debtor. I'll not
be gone very long."

He returned in about fifteen minutes with a Mexican,
who tethered Bud Shannon's horse to the tail of the
chuck wagon, climbed on the seat and drove away.
"And now," said Lee Purdy cheerfully as he started
his motor, "we will vamose."

"Meaning what?"

"Meaning that, it being no longer necessary to set our pace to conform to that of my unfortunate friend's horse, we will make tracks for the Enchanted Hill."

"And what, pray, may the Enchanted Hill be?"

"That is the seat of the Purdy family, Miss Ormsby. I'm the only Purdy who has ever sat on it. All the other Purdys but one think it is the most gosh-awful seat in the world, but it's beautiful to me and I love it; and that, I dare say, is sufficient excuse for the streak of sentiment which prompted me to call it the Enchanted Hill."

"How poetic you are, Mr. Purdy!"

"Not at all. My little sister coined that name for our ranch home. She lives with me at La Cuesta Encantada."

"Indeed!"

"Quite so. And just as a sop to your natural feminine curiosity I will admit now that there is not, nor has there ever been, any Mrs. Lee Purdy."

Gail Ormsby chuckled at his astuteness and joyous frankness.

"So your sister keeps house for you? How nice!"

"Yes, she's queen of the castle. She isn't very well."

"Oh, I'm sorry!"

"Tuberculosis," he explained. "She's just twenty years old and she's been ill two years. But she's getting better on the Enchanted Hill. I'm going to make a hand out of Hallie yet, if she doesn't die of loneliness."